Race Ahead with Reading

The Boy with the Pudding Touch

By Laura North

Illustrated by Neil Chapman

To Charlotte and George - LN

Chapter One

It was the day before Jack's birthday.
He would be nine years old. His dad had
made him a special cake with nine candles
on it.

"Can I have a piece now?" said Jack,
looking at the big cake hungrily.
"No, Jack," said Dad. "You'll have to wait
until tomorrow!"

Jack was annoyed. The cake looked so delicious, and he was very greedy. When his dad wasn't looking, he grabbed a huge slice of cake and stuffed it in his mouth.

"Get upstairs to bed Jack!" shouted his dad. "You're so greedy."

Jack ran up the stairs. He went into his bedroom. Under the bed there was a silver box, glinting in the light.

"I wonder if that's a birthday present for me?" he thought.

He ripped open the silver paper, even though it wasn't his birthday yet. Inside the box was a sparkling gold coin.

There were some words on it: "Touch me and your next wish will come true."

"What a load of rubbish!" said Jack. "I bet nothing happens at all." He held the coin in his hands, and then put it in his pocket and forgot about it. How could a stupid coin make his wishes come true?

Chapter Two

Jack sat down for tea with his mum and dad. All he could see on his plate was a sea of vegetables. "I hate broccoli," said Jack. "And peas and carrots."

But in the middle of the table was a big chocolate mousse, which was for pudding. "Can I have some pudding now, please?" asked Jack.

"No," said his mum. "You have to finish
your broccoli first."

"I hate broccoli!" shouted Jack.

"I wish that I only had to eat puddings.
I wish that everything I touched could turn
into a pudding!" Jack grabbed his broccoli
and threw it onto the table in a tantrum.

Before his parents could shout at him for being so greedy and badly behaved, something magical happened. **ZAP!** Suddenly his broccoli had disappeared.

In its place was a huge pudding. It was a big cream cake, covered in pink icing and raspberries. He stuffed the creamy wonder into his mouth until it had all gone.

11

"My wish came true!" cried Jack, through mouthfuls of cake. He took the coin out of his pocket. It was glowing brightly.

"I can't wait for my birthday now. My life is going to be amazing – all puddings and nothing else!" said Jack.

Chapter Three

The next day, Jack woke up bright and early. "I'm nine years old today and I have a super power!" he said.

He realised that he had a pile of homework to do. "I haven't even started my Maths homework," he groaned.

He picked up his text book.

ZAP! The homework full of

numbers and graphs became

a sundae, with layers of

ice cream, fruit and chocolate.

"I can tell my teacher I ate my homework!" he said as he stuffed the sundae into his mouth, ice cream spilling down his face. "This has to be the best birthday present ever!" he shouted.

There was a knock at the front door.

"Jack!" shouted Mum. "It's Robert.

He's coming up to play a video game."

The boys sat down in front of the TV

to play a game.

But as soon as Jack touched his controller

it turned into a chocolate eclair.

"Oh well," he said licking his fingers.

"What happened?" said Robert, looking

confused.

"The best thing ever," said Jack. "Everything I touch turns into a pudding."

"Right," said Robert.

Jack grabbed Robert's controller.

It turned into another chocolate eclair.

Jack ate that.

"I have to go now," said Robert.

"OK, bye!" called Jack, as Robert walked out

of his bedroom.

Jack had an uneasy feeling. He was feeling a bit sick after eating so many puddings, and wished he could have played the game with his friend.

"Oh well," he said. "I've got my party to look forward to now."

Chapter Four

Jack's mum and dad spent hours getting his

party ready. All of his friends came over.

There were balloons, party games and lots

of brightly wrapped birthday presents all

sitting on the table.

"Here," said his best friend Sarah. "I think you'll love this. I spent ages choosing it." Jack grabbed it. But as soon as he started to rip the wrapping paper off...

ZAP! It turned into a big ice cream covered with chocolate sauce and marshmallows.

Sarah watched in horror. Jack picked up the presents one by one. And each one turned into a different cake or dessert.

"All of my presents are gone," he said. The whole room was stuffed full with puddings, all different sizes and colours.

Sarah looked upset so Jack went to hug her.

But as soon as he touched her, she turned into a green and orange jelly with sugar diamonds on top. His wish had turned the best day of his life into a nightmare.

Chapter Five

"I've turned my best friend into a pudding,"
Jack cried. "I wish I hadn't been so greedy.
I just want her back."

He put Sarah the jelly in the fridge to
make sure no one ate her.

He put his hand in his pocket and pulled out the glittering gold coin. "I wish that things would just go back to the way they were!" he cried.

"I promise I will not be greedy or naughty any more. Just please turn my friend back." The coin glowed in his hand.

Jack crossed his fingers and ran back down the stairs. All his presents were back on the table, though there was a toy car that had some bite marks in it.

He took a deep breath and went to the kitchen. He opened the fridge door slowly. "What am I doing in the fridge?" said Sarah. She climbed out, shivering.

From that day on, Jack wasn't so keen on puddings. And he was very careful about what he wished for.

And the next wish you make, make it one that you won't regret just in case it comes true...

First published in 2013 by
Franklin Watts
338 Euston Road
London
NW1 3BH

Franklin Watts Australia
Level 17/207 Kent Street
Sydney
NSW 2000

Series Editor: Melanie Palmer
Editor: Jackie Hamley
Series Advisor: Catherine Glavina
Series Designer: Peter Scoulding

A CIP catalogue record for this book is
available from the British Library.

ISBN 978 1 4451 2646 3 (hbk)
ISBN 978 1 4451 2652 4 (pbk)
ISBN 978 1 4451 2658 6 (ebook)
ISBN 978 1 4451 2664 7 (library ebook)

Printed in China

Franklin Watts is a division of Hachette
Children's Books, an Hachette UK company.
www.hachette.co.uk